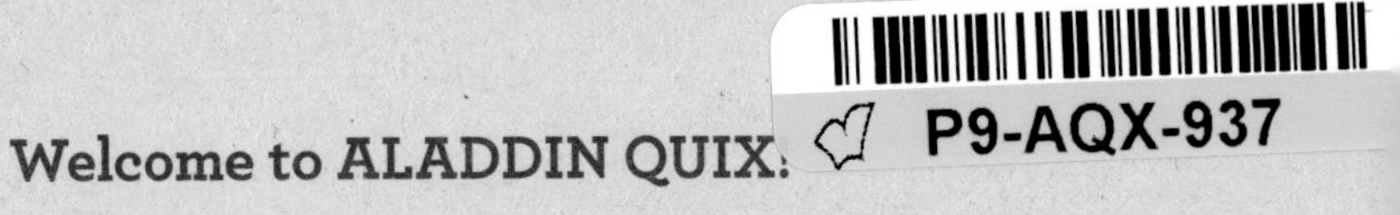

Welcome to ALADDIN QUIX!

If you are looking for fast, fun-to-read stories with colorful characters, lots of kid-friendly humor, easy-to-follow action, entertaining story lines, and lively illustrations, then **ALADDIN QUIX** is for you!

But wait, there's more!

If you're also looking for stories with tables of contents; word lists; about-the-book questions; 64, 80, or 96 pages; short chapters; short paragraphs; and large fonts, then **ALADDIN QUIX** is *definitely* for you!

ALADDIN QUIX: The next step between ready to reads and longer, more challenging chapter books, for readers five to eight years old.

Read the other books in the Pet Pals series!

Mitzy's Homecoming

Luna's Obedience School

Buttons's Talent Show

PET PALS

Gus's Escape

by ALLISON GUTKNECHT

illustrated by ANJA GROTE

ALADDIN QUIX

New York London Toronto Sydney New Delhi

ALADDIN QUIX
An imprint of Simon & Schuster Children's Publishing Division
1230 Avenue of the Americas, New York, New York 10020
First Aladdin QUIX paperback edition May 2023

Also available in an Aladdin QUIX hardcover edition.

Series designed by Laura Lyn DiSiena
Cover designed by Alicia Mikles
Interior designed by Ginny Kemmerer
The illustrations for this book were rendered digitally.
The text of this book was set in Archer Medium.
Manufactured in the United States of America 0323 OFF
2 4 6 8 10 9 7 5 3 1
Library of Congress Control Number 2022944488
ISBN 978-1-5344-7408-6 (hc)
ISBN 978-1-5344-7407-9 (pbk)
ISBN 978-1-5344-7409-3 (ebook)

For Oakley,

my sassy and sweet sunshine

Cast of Characters

Buttons (BUH-tens): Shy kitten at Whiskers Down the Lane Animal Shelter

Mitzy (MIT-zee): Excitable toy poodle at the shelter

Luna (LOO-nuh): Cranky cat at the shelter

Gus (GUS): Large guard dog at the shelter

Ted (TED): Manager of the shelter

Dustin (DUSS-ten): Young boy and friend of Mitzy's

Contents

Chapter 1: Runaway 1

Chapter 2: Into the Woods 14

Chapter 3: Leap of Faith 21

Chapter 4: A Friendly Face 33

Chapter 5: Helping Hands 42

Chapter 6: Family Friends 50

Word List 63

Questions 65

1

Runaway

"Can cats get sunburnt?" **Buttons** asks. He squints up at the harsh rays of light, and the centers of his amber eyes turn to thin black slits. "I'm not sure I like Ted's plan."

"Why? We get to be outside!" **Mitzy** says. She rolls over and wiggles against the ground. "I love outside."

"You're going to get dirty!" **Luna** yells at her. "No one wants a white poodle covered in grass stains."

"I agree with Buttons," **Gus** says. He paces in circles, tangling his leash around the leg of a table. "It's **dangerous** to leave us out here by ourselves."

"By ourselves? There are volunteers all over this yard," Luna points out. "And by the way, I haven't hissed at any of them." More quietly she mumbles, "Yet."

"They're strangers," Gus states. "Strangers are the outdoor version of intruders." He lifts his snout in the air and sniffs, checking the new people's scents.

"I don't understand," Buttons says. "Why would bringing us to the front lawn make people want to adopt us?" Buttons tries to cuddle against Luna in the cage they're sharing, and Luna slides away.

"Because they can see us from the street as they drive by," Luna explains. "And Ted thinks that will make people more likely to stop and meet us."

Buttons scoots closer to Luna

again, squashing them both in a corner.

Luna twitches her whiskers. “Can’t you move over? Just because Ted put us in here together doesn’t mean you have to sit on top of me.”

Buttons shuffles away, but

keeps his tail draped over Luna. "Sorry, I was chilly," he says. "I'm not used to fresh air."

"Fresh air is amazing!" Mitzy exclaims. "It is why I like to go on walks with Dustin when he visits me."

"You like to go because he gives you treats," Luna corrects her. "It has nothing to do with the air."

Gus continues to spin around the table, wrapping his leash more and more tightly.

"Gus, you are going to get

dizzy," Mitzy tells him. "Come onto the grass with me."

"I need to stay on **patrol**," Gus insists. "You never know who might pose a threat."

Luna thumps her tail twice. "You look like the mutt version of a merry-go-round," she tells him.

"I am not a mutt!" Gus argues. "I am a guard dog!"

"Wheeeeeee!" Mitzy buries her cheeks in the green blades of grass and starts to dig. "Outside is so much fun!"

“I can’t believe I’m about to say this,” Luna begins, “but, Gus, be more like Mitzy.”

“Yes! I am the best!” Mitzy agrees.

Gus stops walking and stares at Luna. “What do you mean?” he asks.

“Relax,” Luna says. “Enjoy life.

Stop acting like you have to be tough all the time."

Gus scans the parking lot, then tucks his tail between his legs. "I'm not sure I know how to relax," he admits.

"You need a toy," Buttons suggests. "Mitzy has her squeaky purple ball. Luna had her mouse, which she gave to me. What's your favorite toy?"

Gus stares at his toes sadly. "I never had a toy I loved."

"Never?" Mitzy is shocked.

"That is terrible news."

"It's okay," Gus says. "I never knew what to do with one."

"You play with it!" Mitzy says. "You chew and you squeak and you run and you fetch and you throw and you squeeze and you—"

"He gets the idea," Luna says, cutting her off.

Just then **Ted** exits Whiskers Down the Lane with a blanket-draped cage. He carries it down the driveway and places it on the ground.

"What is that?" Gus asks nervously.

"Maybe it's a bird," Buttons says. "I've always wanted to see a bird up close."

"This shelter doesn't have birds," Luna says.

Ted grips the center of the blanket with his fingers and raises it slowly. Piece by piece the creature in the cage comes into view: tiny nose, short whiskers, pointy face, beady eyes, round ears.

"No!" Gus barks at his highest

pitch. “No, NO, NOOOOOOO!” He pulls against his leash until it is stretched as thinly as a strand of floss.

“Calm down, Gus!” Mitzy pleads.

Gus jumps to the right. Then he jerks to the left. His leash strains to hold him in place.

“It’s okay!” Buttons echoes. “It’s only a big—”

SNAP!

Gus’s leash breaks in half, and he takes off across the lawn toward the side of the building. He rounds the corner, faster, faster, until he's out of sight.

2

Into the Woods

“What do we do?” Buttons cries. “Someone has to catch him!”

“Ted will,” Luna promises, but she sounds unsure—because Ted’s back is to them, and none of the

volunteers have noticed Gus's escape.

"Why did he do that?" Mitzy asks. "He knows better than to run away."

"He got spooked," Buttons explains. "By the giant mouse. Gus hates mice."

"I believe that's a rat," Luna corrects him. "But close enough."

Buttons jingles the lock of their cage. "Somebody must go after him." He slides the latch to the side slowly, carefully, until it unhinges. "Are you coming?"

"Okay," Luna agrees, and she pushes the door open.

"You cannot both go!" Mitzy protests. "You cannot leave me alone. And I am tied here." The three of them glance at Mitzy's leash, which is still attached to the table.

"You stay with Mitzy," Buttons tells Luna. "I'll go."

"Are you positive?" Luna asks.

"I'm older and bigger and meaner. Maybe you should stay with Mitzy and I should—"

But before Luna can finish, Buttons bounds to the ground. "I can be brave," he assures them.

Then he dashes in the direction where Gus had **disappeared**.

"Gus?" Buttons calls softly.

The kitten stands at the line of trees behind Whiskers Down the Lane, staring into the shadowy woods. **Cautiously** he takes three steps forward, his small paws crinkling the dry leaves.

"Gus?" he tries again.

He skulks forward a few more paces and then stops.

COOOOOOOO. COOOOOOOO.

In the distance he hears a flock of birds fly overhead. A cool wind breezes across the tip of his tail. He shudders slightly, glancing behind him at the roof of the shelter. It would be so easy to return, to go back to Luna and

Mitzy and everything he knows.

But what about Gus?

CAW, CAW.

MeeeeeEEP. MeeeeeEEP.

Nisssssssst.

Spooky sounds surround him everywhere, but still, Buttons doesn't leave.

"Gus?" he calls.

Keeping his eyes focused on the path ahead, Buttons continues into the woods.

3

Leap of Faith

"What if they never come back?" Mitzy whimpers. She has stopped playing in the grass and is crouching under the table beneath Luna's cage. Her long ears hang forward on either side of her face like curtains.

"They will," Luna declares, but she sounds less certain than usual.

"How do you know?" Mitzy asks.

Luna stretches her front legs, and her claws catch the edge of the table. "I guess I don't, but I do know that worrying won't make them return any faster," she replies.

Mitzy lies down and rests her chin on top of her feet, her deep brown eyes droopy with concern.

"What should I do instead of worry?" she asks.

Luna studies one of her paws. Then she begins picking at her toes with her teeth. "Roll around in the grass," she suggests.

"I do not feel like it," Mitzy argues.

Luna extends her nails and examines the points. "Chase your tail," she tries again.

"I do not want to," Mitzy protests.

With a heavy sigh Luna lowers

her head to peer below the table. Mitzy perks up at the sight of her friend.

"This is a once-in-a-lifetime

offer," Luna says. "Do you want to clean my ears?"

"Yes! Yes!" Mitzy launches to her feet, her tail a sudden flurry of excitement. "I would like to very much! I am sure they are filthy."

"Fine," Luna agrees. She hops down and settles beside Mitzy. "Go ahead."

Mitzy sloshes her tongue into Luna's ear and licks happily. Luna sits grimacing, but she doesn't complain.

"I am excellent at grooming

cats," Mitzy says, complimenting herself, just as Ted turns around and spots them.

"Hey!" he exclaims. "Luna, what are you doing out of your cage?" He strides toward them with wide, frantic steps. "And where are Gus and Buttons?"

Gus didn't realize how much he missed running. He **gallops** freely through the trees without being held back by a leash, or a cage, or a person. He loves the feeling of the wind on his skin, the dirt beneath his paws, and the sense of adventure.

He runs until the outline of Whiskers Down the Lane vanishes through the treetops. He runs until the sight of that giant mouse is banished from his mind.

He runs until he is lost.

He stops sprinting in the

middle of a clearing. His dry tongue dangles out of his mouth. He pants heavily and inspects his surroundings, searching for a familiar sight.

Which path did he take to get here?

Which path is the way out?

Which path will lead him to a drink of water?

He starts to jog in the direction that looks brightest, growing thirstier and thirstier the farther he travels. Finally the trees thin out and patches of sky come into view. Up ahead a tall apartment building appears.

And on its patio Gus spots a small **inflatable** swimming pool. Water!

A fence separates the border of the woods from the building's

property. Gus balances on his rear legs to measure the fence's height. Then he lowers himself to the ground, backs up, and inhales a deep breath.

He takes off. His paws pound the earth as he picks up speed. The fence's wooden slats get closer and closer, clearer and clearer. Gus focuses his eyes, readies his legs, and prepares to take a gigantic leap.

SCREECH!

At the last moment before

jumping, Gus changes his mind. He skids across the leaves and slides into the fence with an enormous BANG.

"Yow!" he wails.

A red gash forms on his right

leg where it hit the hard planks.

"YOW!" he hollers again.

But no matter how loudly he yelps, there doesn't seem to be anybody around to hear him.

4

A Friendly Face

Gus cleans his wound with his tongue, licking the cut over and over as his mouth grows even drier.

With his leg throbbing, he teeters up and down the length of

the fence, searching for an opening. When he finds none, he turns back toward the woods and limps forward. One step, and then another, paw by paw.

"Owww," he moans pitifully. He collapses beside the curved roots of a tree to take a break. Then he gazes up to the sky and howls.

"Gus?"

His name, as soft as a whisper, travels to his ears. Gus snaps his head to the side and peers

between the tree trunks. The branches above him **rustle** in the wind, but the rest of the woods has turned silent.

He must be hearing things. The pain from his leg has to be playing tricks on his mind.

"Gus?"

The word, sharper this time, greets him like a warm smile. Gus stands up weakly.

"Who is it?" he calls into the breeze. He sniffs heavily at the air to track the scent.

"It's me!" the small voice answers him.

Gus takes another enormous whiff, and his eyes widen with surprise. "Buttons?" Gus calls. "How did you find me?"

"I haven't found you yet," Buttons's voice answers. "I don't see you. Can you walk toward me?"

Gus takes a step, but his leg **buckles** beneath him. "I—I cannot right now," he stammers.

"Where are you?" Buttons asks. "Are you okay?"

"I am . . ." Gus glances down at the deep scrape. "I am fine, yes." His voice **quavers** slightly.

"You don't sound fine," Buttons tells him. "Bark so I can find you."

Gus sits, his hurt leg dangling in front of him. "WOOF. WOOF."

"Keep going!" Buttons encourages him. "I think I'm getting closer."

"WOOF. WOOF, WOOF,

WOOF." Gus's throat itches. "WOOF." His mouth feels like sandpaper. "Buttons?" he calls faintly.

No response.

Gus hobbles a few paces using only three legs, before stopping to listen. "Buttons?" he calls again.

Nothing.

Gus places all four feet on the ground, which makes him screech with pain. Just then Buttons bursts through the nearby bushes.

"Oh my goodness!" the kitten exclaims. "What happened?"

"I am fine," Gus says shakily. "It is merely a scratch."

Buttons studies the cut and pats Gus's leg gently. "Can you walk?"

"Of course," Gus assures him,

but he doesn't try to prove it. "I—I just could use some water first."

"Yes, you need a drink," Buttons agrees. "You ran a long way."

"There's a pool by that building." Gus stares toward the patio. "That's where I was going when I . . . I . . ."

"When you had an accident," Buttons fills in. "Accidents happen." He looks toward the apartment windows. "Stay here and rest. I'm going to find help."

“I don’t need help,” Gus insists. “I am fine.”

Buttons raises himself like a ladder until he and Gus are nose to nose. “Everybody needs help sometimes, Gus,” Buttons tells him. “Even guard dogs.”

5

Helping Hands

Buttons shimmies between the fence's slats and scurries to the empty patio. He rounds the apartment building, searching for someone to assist Gus. In the distance he hears a bouncing ball,

and he rushes in the direction of the sound. When he reaches the curb, he spots a basketball net across the street, and a boy dribbling in front of it.

"MEOW!" Buttons calls in his loudest voice. "MEOWWWWW."

The boy doesn't turn.

Buttons sprints to a parked car and leaps onto its hood, and then to its roof.

"MEOWWWWWWWWWW!" he tries again.

The boy holds the ball still.

"MEOW! MEOW! MEOW!" Buttons mews until the boy spins to face him.

The boy squints and scans the kitten, and his eyebrows jolt up his forehead. "Buttons?" he greets the cat. "Is that you?" He dashes across the street with the ball smushed against his ribs.

As the boy comes closer, Buttons's short tail springs to attention. It's Mitzy's friend **Dustin**! He'll be able to take care of Gus—Buttons is sure of it.

"Are you lost?" Dustin asks when he gets to the car.

"MEOW!" Buttons cries. He dives from the roof onto the sidewalk.

"Did you get locked out of the shelter?" Dustin asks. He bends to pick up Buttons, but the kitten dodges his grip and runs toward the woods.

"MEOW!" Buttons calls behind him. "MEOW!"

"Come back here," Dustin begs him. "I'll carry you home."

"MEOWWWWWWWWWW," Buttons protests.

Dustin, confused, jogs after Buttons. He follows the kitten around the building, through the yard, and across the patio, until finally they reach the fence.

"Gus!" Buttons calls as he races

ahead. “I found Dustin—you know, the boy who comes to walk Mitzy? He can help.”

Buttons slinks between the slats of the fence. He dashes to Gus, who is still crumpled beside a tree root, his hurt leg lying at an angle.

“MEOW!” Buttons alerts Dustin.

The boy peers over the top of the fence. “Gus, oh no!” Dustin pushes himself up and over.

Gus lifts his chin slightly. The world around him looks fuzzy,

like everything is spinning in place. Dustin kneels beside him. He studies the cut and then scratches the fur between Gus's ears.

"We'll get you fixed up," Dustin promises. "Buttons, stay with Gus. I'll be right back. Don't worry."

"I was not worried," Gus says softly as Dustin climbs back over the fence. "Guard dogs do not worry."

Buttons curls up next to him to wait. "Then, I was worried enough for both of us," he confesses.

6

Family Friends

Ted made an effort to return Luna to her cage, but she put up such a fight that he eventually allowed her to remain under the table beside Mitzy.

The poodle lets out a miserable

sigh. "Why is Mr. Ted not out looking for Gus and Buttons?" she asks Luna.

"He sent volunteers after them," Luna explains. "Plus, now he's inside finding your ball so that you'll stop whining."

"I am too sad about Gus and Buttons to play right now," Mitzy says. She **nuzzles** her face against Luna's fur and lets out another whimper.

In front of them, a minivan pulls into the lot and rolls into a parking spot. Its side door slides open, and Mitzy sits up straighter as a familiar sneaker steps onto the pavement.

"Dustin?" She vaults to her feet and her tail wags wildly. "Luna, Dustin is here!"

Dustin reaches into the van, and when he turns back, a small fuzzy head is poking through the bend of his elbow.

"Look who I found!" he calls, hurrying across the yard.

"Buttons! Hooray!" Mitzy exclaims. "But what about Gus?"

Dustin places the kitten in the open cage and strokes Mitzy's neck. Then he heads back toward the minivan.

"Excuse me!" Mitzy calls after him. "Gus is still missing!"

"Gus is here too," Buttons promises. "He just needs some extra help." The three watch as Dustin and his mom guide Gus out of the van, his front leg wrapped in a clean white bandage.

"You found him!" Mitzy calls happily.

"I can't believe it," Luna agrees. "Buttons, I didn't think you had it in you."

"It wasn't easy," Buttons admits. "But I tried to be brave. Just like you taught me."

With Dustin's support Gus limps over to his friends.

"What happened to you?" Luna asks.

"I—I hurt myself," Gus says, sounding ashamed. "But Dustin patched me up."

Luna stares at Dustin curiously, like she is seeing him for the first time.

"Um, is she going to swipe at me again?" Dustin asks **suspiciously**. He tiptoes backward under Luna's steely gaze.

Luna narrows her eyes and marches toward him.

"Luna, don't!" Buttons warns. He dives to the ground to try to block her path, but Luna swerves around him.

"No, Luna!" Mitzy begs. She strains forward, but her leash holds her in place. "Do not bite Dustin! Stop!"

But Luna doesn't stop.

Instead she walks right up to Dustin's bony ankle. She studies it for one second, two seconds, three. . . .

Then she pushes her cheek against his shin, and ever so slowly Luna rubs her whiskers against him.

"Thank you," she purrs.

Surprised, Dustin reaches down and taps the top of Luna's head. "You like me now?" he asks.

She ducks away from his fingers but does not snarl. "Let's not get carried away," she states. She strolls back to the table as Ted exits Whiskers

Down the Lane, clutching Mitzy's ball in his fist.

"No way!" he shouts. "You found them!" He rushes over and tosses the ball aside. "Where were they?"

"It's kind of a long story," Dustin begins.

While Ted listens to Dustin, Gus glances around the yard nervously. "By any chance," he starts, "did that . . . thing go back inside?"

"The rat?" Luna asks. "It got adopted. So now you have no more excuses for running away."

Mitzy flicks her ears toward Gus. “Do not ever do that again!” she scolds him.

“I’m sorry,” Gus says. “Sometimes I have trouble staying calm.”

“That’s why you need a toy,” Buttons says. “A toy can help you relax.”

“Here,” Mitzy says, nudging her ball toward Gus. “You can borrow this.”

“Really?” Gus asks. “But you love your ball.”

“I do, because it is fun and it is

noisy," Mitzy agrees. "But I can still share it."

Gus grips the ball in his teeth and gives it a loud **SQUEAK**.

"See how fun that is?" Mitzy asks.

"I do," Gus tells her. "Thank you."

"Ted?" a volunteer calls from across the lawn. "This family would like to take Dolly."

Mitzy sighs at the news. "Dolly is getting a home, and we are not," she moans.

"Maybe someday we will,"

Buttons says hopefully. “And for now we have each other. Having friends is almost as good as having a family, right?”

“Nah,” Luna replies.

“It’s not?” Gus asks.

“No,” Luna tells them. “Friends are better. A family is chosen for you. But a friend, you choose for yourself.”

The four friends sit facing one another as they think this over, their eight front paws forming an unbroken circle.

They may not yet have been adopted, but at least they know that they have already been chosen.

Word List

buckles (BUH•kuls): Collapses

cautiously (KAW•shuss•lee): Carefully

dangerous (DANE•juh•russ): Able or likely to cause harm

disappeared (diss•uh•PEERED): Vanished from sight

gallops (GA•luhps): Runs fast

inflatable (in•FLAY•tuh•bull): Capable of being blown up with air

nuzzles (NUH•zulls): Rubs gently

patrol (puh•TROLL): The action of walking around an area to guard it

quavers (KWAY•verz): Shakes

rustle (RUH•sull): Make a series of small sounds

suspiciously (suh•SPIH•shuss•lee): Distrustfully

Questions

1. What did Gus see that caused him to run away?
2. What is surprising about Buttons being the one to chase after Gus?
3. How did Gus injure himself?
4. In what ways are the four pet pals alike? In what ways are they different from one another?
5. Have you ever made friends with someone unexpected? Talk about your friendship.

6. Who do you think will be adopted first: Mitzy, Luna, Buttons, or Gus? Why?

Our Principal Is a Frog!
MACK RHINO
PRIVATE EYE
The Big Race-Lace Case
ROYAL SWEETS
A Royal Rescue
Helen Perelman
The Adventures of
ALLIE and AMY
The Best Friend Plan
EXPRESS TRAIN TO TROUBLE
ROBERT QUACKENBUSH
Pet Pals

CHUCKLE YOUR WAY THROUGH THESE EASY-TO-READ ILLUSTRATED CHAPTER BOOKS!

EBOOK EDITIONS ALSO AVAILABLE

FROM ALADDIN
SIMONANDSCHUSTER.COM/KIDS